WHISPERS OF LOVE

AARUSHI PANDEYA

INDIA • SINGAPORE • MALAYSIA

Acknowledgement

I am profoundly grateful for the unwavering support and love from my family, whose encouragement has been the bedrock of my creative journey.

My heartfelt appreciation goes to the entire publishing team for their guidance and expertise, transforming my manuscript into a polished work of art.

I extend my deepest gratitude to my readers, whose enthusiasm and feedback continue to inspire and drive my passion for storytelling.

Finally, I owe a debt of gratitude to the countless authors whose words have shaped and influenced my own. Your work is a constant source of inspiration.

Thank you for being a part of this incredible journey.

Sincerely,

Aarushi Pandeya

"Dedicated to my grand parents and parents"

Contents

Chapter – 1

The Last First Day

"ring! ring! ring!"

The alarm blared on the phone, causing Adelaide to stir in her sleep. Her eyes slowly opened, and she removed the blanket from over her face. She at once sat up, for it was her first day in the last year of the high school. The first thing she did was to hit the 'off' button of the ringing alarm on her phone.

Adelaide was an extremely beautiful girl of around eighteen years of age, with slim and attractive figure, wavy, brown hair that reached upto her waist, dreamy green eyes with long eyelashes, pale complexion, and soft looking pink lips.

The door of Adelaide's room then flew open to reveal her younger sister, sixteen year old Amelia. She was just as pretty as her older sister, with slim and attractive figure, straight, blonde hair that reached upto her shoulders, brown eyes with long eyelashes, pale complexion, and soft looking pink lips.

Finding Adelaide awake, she said, "Oh, so you're awake."

"Just tell me why wouldn't I be awake?", Adelaide said. "After all, it's the first day of the last year at high school!"

"Yeah, yeah, I know.", Amelia said. "No need to rub it in."

"Now get out, I have to get ready.", Adelaide said, ushering her sister out of the room.

"Wait!", Amelia said.

"What now?", Adelaide said.

"All the best for the first day in twelfth grade!", Amelia said.

"You could have told me this downstairs!", Adelaide said, and closed the door behind her.

"I still can't believe this is our last year in school.", Olivia said. "I mean, it feels like just yesterday we were in the third grade, listening to Mrs Peterson lecture about the solar system."

"I know, right?", Adelaide said. "And there is so much for looking forward to, like the yearbook, the prom, the graduation ceremony."

"And the fact that it's seven-thirty and we still haven't collected our class schedules yet!", Olivia said, looking at her watch.

The girls looked at each other, and without uttering another word, made a run for the school reception.

Chapter – 2

The Famous Son of the Famous Doctor

Upon reaching her classroom, Adelaide was all out of breath. But fortunately for her, Mr Wilson hadn't reached yet, and unexpectedly, nor had anyone else.

"Huh?", Adelaide said.

She thought of all possible places where her classmates could be. But since the first class was that of the language French designated in the exact room which she was currently in, she couldn't think of any other place.

"Most importantly, where's Olivia?", Adelaide thought. "She was with me a few minutes ago."

Just then, Olivia entered the room in the exact same manner her best friend had entered ; all out of breath.

"What…are…you…doing…here?", Olivia managed to say in between heaving breaths.

"What do you mean by 'what are you doing here'?", Adelaide said. "Obviously wondering where has everybody gone."

"You don't know?", Olivia said.

"Know what?", Adelaide said.

"Dellie, everyone in the school knows that the son of none other than Dr Raymond Wellington has come to our school for a whole year!", Olivia said excitedly.

"Wait, Raymond Wellington as in, the Yale graduate of 1993?", Adelaide said.

"Yes!", Olivia said. "The one and only Julian Wellington is coming to our school! Can you believe it?"

"So that's what the crowd in the main lobby was for.", Adelaide said. "But what about the teachers? Surely they wouldn't be so crazy about a student."

"They aren't.", a male's voice said.

Adelaide and Olivia turned around to find an extremely handsome boy of around the same age as them. The boy had short, straight, jet black hair, dark blue eyes, pale complexion, with his face devoid of any facial hair. He had the perfect body, with broad shoulders, and six pack abs would definitely be there underneath his shirt. The boy was standing with his arms crossed, and leaning against the classroom door, with a charming smile on his face.

"They are all in the teacher's lounge.", the boy said.

"Julian Wellington?", Olivia said, unable to believe that she was standing just a few metres away from him.

"Let me guess, the teachers are in the teacher's lounge as they are waiting for the crowd gathered for you to settle down, am I right?, Adelaide said.

As a result, Olivia gently hit Adelaide on the elbow, gesturing her to talk nicely to the famous doctor's son.

Hearing Adelaide's question, Julian chuckled softly, then said, "Yes, but I'm not proud of this incident, okay?"

"Yeah, whatever.", Adelaide said, and rolled her eyes.

"Avery, look! It's Julian Wellington!", a girl from behind Julian exclaimed.

Julian turned around to find the most popular girl in the school, Avery Campbell, along with her gang. Avery was a beautiful, but arrogant girl who had wavy, dirty-blonde hair held in a half pony tail, chocolate brown eyes, fair complexion, and pink lips.

"Oh no, not again.", Adelaide whispered, rolling her eyes.

"So, you're in this class?", Avery said.

"Yeah.", Julian said.

"Oh great!", Adelaide whispered in a sarcastic tone.

"Great!", Avery said, and extended her hand towards Julian. "I am Avery by the way, Avery Campbell."

"Nice to meet you Avery, I am Julian Wellington.", Julian said, accepting her hand.

"Oh, I know who you are.", Avery said. "Everybody knows."

"Well, what can I say?", Julian said, and playfully shrugged his shoulders, which irritated Adelaide even more.

Chapter – 3

The Almost Accident

A week later in calculus

"Ugh!", Adelaide said. "Why am I not able to solve this?

"Which question are you on?", Olivia said.

"Eighteenth.", Adelaide replied. "What about you?"

"I'm still stuck on sixteenth.", Olivia said. "Honestly speaking, eighteenth is actually a tough one."

Just then, Julian, who was sitting behind Adelaide, said, "Hey, I couldn't help but overhear. If you want, I can help you."

"Yes, please. She has been stuck at this problem for like, forever.", Olivia said at once, preventing Adelaide to say anything further.

One day, while the French language class was in full motion, the sound of a loud thud came from just outside the room, startling everyone in there, along with others who were in the rooms located close to the first one.

"What the…", Olivia said.

"Sounds like something big fell down.", one of the students said.

"I'll go check.", Adelaide said.

Upon going outside her classroom, she found that the medium-sized painting made by one of the alums of the school was on the floor, instead of it's original position, which was just above the classroom.

"When was this painting put up?", Adelaide said, examining the wall from where the painting had fallen, while standing on a chair.

"Just a few days before the commencement of this academic year.", Mr Wilson replied.

"So that explains it.", Adelaide said. "The nail upon which the hook of the painting had been hung wasn't properly drilled into the wall, and due to the weight of the painting, the nail gave away."

"So what do you think we should do now?", Mr Wilson said.

"If you permit, I can try.", Adelaide said. "I mean, I'm already standing in that position."

"But how will you do it?", Mr Wilson said. "We have no tools."

"We can bring one from the wooden lab.", Julian said.

"Are you okay there?", Olivia said.

"Yeah.", Adelaide replied, still on the chair. "It's just that, the nail comes out, no matter how much I try to drill it in."

Saying this, Adelaide came on her toes, trying to get a better view of the nail. Just then, the chair started stumbling, and Adelaide lost her balance. As she was about to hit the hard floor, she felt a strong and steady pair of arms catch her, preventing her from falling any further. It all happened in an instant, so fast that Adelaide was all out of breath.

Upon realizing that she had been saved, Adelaide opened her tightly shut eyes to look at her saviour. The first thing she saw was Julian's dreamy dark blue eyes. With his face so close to hers, she could make out each and every detail of his face, which she now found to be so perfect ; well defined, chiseled, and sharp features. Her hands were on his muscular chest, and she could feel his racing heartbeat.

Julian looked at the girl in his arms. Her eyes were astonishingly beautiful ; nature's green, with long eyelashes, and with her face so close to his, he could make out each and every detail of her perfect face ; her sharp nose, and her soft looking pink lips.

"Oh my God!", Olivia said, pulling Julian and Adelaide out of their respective trances. "Dellie, are you okay?"

"Uh, um, yeah…yes.", Adelaide said, and removed her hand from Julian's chest, while he put her down.

"Are you sure? I mean, look at you, you are still panting.", Julian said, and stood close to Adelaide for support.

"I think it will be better if we take her to the infirmary.", Olivia said.

"What? No!", Adelaide said. "I'm perfectly fine!"

"She said she is fine, alright?", Avery said, no longer able to see Julian standing so close to Adelaide.

"Avery, she almost hit her head.", Olivia said. "We can't just leave her like that."

"But she didn't, right?", Avery said. "So what are you all making so much fuss about?"

"Avery, stop being such a baby.", Julian said, calmly.

"I…I… I'm not being a baby!", Avery said, and stormed off.

Chapter – 4

The Confrontation

A few days before Adelaide's almost accident, Julian helped Adelaide solve a complex calculus problem she was stuck on, just because Olivia hadn't given a chance to Adelaide when he had asked if he could help them, by abruptly answering 'yes' to him. And Adelaide was somewhat glad that her best friend had done so, for her irritation for the Yale graduate's son was reducing day by day, as she initially had an impression that he was a playboy. But by observing his kind nature towards everybody, her thoughts about him being a playboy slowly started to diminish.

A day after Adelaide fell off the chair and almost hit her head, she decided to go to the school field at the end of the day, for she knew that she would find Julian there, as he had been practicing with his football teammates everyday since the school started ; for nearly a month.

Upon reaching the field, she found Avery and her friends already there, with Avery obviously waiting for Julian to complete his practice. Nonetheless, Adelaide found a seat for herself on the stairs, away from Avery and her group. But unfortunately, Avery's glance fell on Adelaide, and the arrogant girl at once went over to her, gesturing for her group to stay put. It seemed that she wanted to have a personal talk with Adelaide, after all.

"Who do you think you are, huh?", Avery said.

"Excuse me?", Adelaide said.

"Oh, look at you acting all innocent!", Avery said.

Adelaide sighed, then said, "Just tell me already."

"You know very well what I'm here for!", Avery said. "Boyfriend stealer!"

"What the…", Adelaide said, and stood up. "I didn't *steal* your boyfriend! I don't even know who is your boyfriend!"

"No need to act now, Matthews.", Avery said. "I know you fell purposefully off that chair yesterday just so you could get all comfy in Julian's arms!"

"Enough, Avery!", Julian's voice came from behind her, before Adelaide could say something about the false accusation.

Avery turned around to find Julian with his brows furrowed, and his fists clenched. Rest of his team, Avery's group, and others also started gathering to see what was the matter.

"Oh good, you are here.", Avery said. "Tell her you are my boyfriend, not hers!"

Julian unclenched his fists and looked at Adelaide, who looked back at him, with a tensed look on her face.

Turning towards Avery, he said, "Avery, when exactly did I ask you to be my girlfriend?"

"Uh, um……", Avery staggered.

"Okay, you may not have the answer to that.", Julian said. "But I'm sure you have the answer to this one, since, you know, I'm your *boyfriend*. Tell me, when exactly did *you* ask me to be your boyfriend?"

Avery couldn't even stagger this time. No words came out of her mouth.

"So that explains it.", Julian said. "Neither I asked you to be my girlfriend, nor you asked me to be your boyfriend. So how does that make me your boyfriend?"

"Uh….", Avery began, then cleared her throat. "You hung out with me for the past month."

"That doesn't mean we are in a relationship!", Julian said. "And for your information, Adelaide won't do what you accused her of. She doesn't even like me."

"That's not completely true.", Adelaide said timidly, making everyone around her face her. "I mean, yeah, I didn't have a very good impression of you at first, but now, it's different. I just came here to thank you for saving me yesterday."

"You still can't have him!", Avery said.

"Why can't she?", Julian said. "Because for all I know, I'm never gonna be in a relationship with a girl who is as arrogant and bratty as you!"

"Okay, I think that's enough.", Adelaide said. "This discussion is over!"

"Adelaide is right.", Julian said. "It's over."

But when nobody moved from their place, Julian and Adelaide said in unison, "Over, I said!"

At once, Avery turned around, and pushing the people from out of her way, stormed off like she did yesterday, upon being called a baby.

The crowd soon dispersed, except Adelaide and Julian.

Adelaide sat down on the stairs, her head in her hands.

"Um, do you mind if I….", Julian said, gesturing towards the empty place beside Adelaide.

"Yeah, sure.", she said, still holding her head.

"This can't be happening.", Adelaide said, followed by little sobs.

"Whoa! Are you crying?", Julian said.

"N…n…no.", Adelaide said, quickly wiping off her tears.

"It's alright.", Julian said, and kept his hand on Adelaide's shoulder. "Cry all you want. I won't judge….at all. Vent all your feelings…..get angry.

This would help you feel better. Moreover, there is nobody here, only you and me."

Adelaide at once wrapped her arms around Julian, and hugged him.

"I don't know why this happens to me!", Adelaide said between her sobs.

Julian too wrapped his hands around her, reciprocating the hug.

"I thought…..I thought that this last year would be so great. But no, why would it be, when the starting alone has told me that it's gonna be the exact opposite!", Adelaide said.

"Hey, that's not true.", Julian said, wiping off her tears and taking her face in his hands. "This year will be great, trust me."

"How can you be so sure?", Adelaide said.

"Another person can't decide your future, Adelaide.", Julian said. "You are certain about an awful year because of that spoiled and arrogant Avery, aren't you?"

No words came out of Adelaide's mouth. Instead, the sobbing continued.

"Well then you shouldn't be.", Julian said, and hugged her again.

"But she is the most popular girl in school!", Adelaide said, and faced Julian.

"I think you are forgetting who's the most popular boy in school.", Julian said, and winked, which made a little smile appear on Adelaide's lips.

"That's my girl!", Julian said.

Then, while bringing his hands together and gently cupping Adelaide's face, with the hands going through her silky, brown hair, he leaned in towards her, and brought his lips in contact with her lips. Adelaide's arms automatically wrapped around Julian, reciprocating his passionate kiss gently.

Chapter – 5
The Confessions

After a few seconds, Adelaide realized what she had been doing, leading to her abruptly ending the kiss between her and Julian.

"No no no! This can't be happening!", Adelaide said. "I did the exact same thing which Avery accused me of!"

Wiping her tears, she stood up, threw the bag over her shoulder, and just when she was about to take a step forward, she felt a strong hand gently grab her wrist.

"Julian, let me go.", Adelaide said.

"Don't worry, I'll let you go.", Julian said, stepping in front of her to face her. "But I have to tell you this."

"What is it?", Adelaide said.

Sighing, Julian smiled, then said, " Adelaide, you know, I used to believe that love at first sight is a myth. But….when I first saw you, it was like, my heart skipped a beat, and……"

"And?", Adelaide said, the butterflies in her stomach about to take flight any moment.

"And felt that the world fell away beneath my feet.", Julian said, making the butterflies in Adelaide's stomach take flight in full speed. "But being a non-believer in *love at first sight*, I simply deemed it to be a crush."

Adelaide opened her mouth to speak, but was stopped by Julian when he kept his hand on her mouth.

"Wait, let me finish.", Julian said.

"As the days passed, my feelings for you grew stronger. No matter how much I tried to suppress them, they just….grew.", Julian said. "But when you fell from that chair, I felt like my heart skipped a beat, and not in a good way this time."

"And then, when I looked into your eyes, I swear they transported me to a whole new world. And that's when I knew, I was in love with you Adelaide Grace Matthews.", Julian said.

Adelaide looked at Julian, unable to utter even a single word. Just like Julian, when he had first laid eyes on her, Adelaide felt like her heart had skipped a beat the moment Julian uttered those magical words.

"I...I...", Adelaide managed to utter with great difficulty. But that was all she was going to say. Next moment, Adelaide lowered her gaze, and turned her back towards Julian.

"Take all the time you need, okay?", he said, and Adelaide could then hear the footsteps receding into the background.

The next day

Upon finding Olivia in front of her locker, without her best friend, Avery went over and tapped her on her shoulder.

Olivia, who was on her phone talking to someone, turned around and her expression changed from that of cheerfulness to anger.

"I'm gonna call you later.", Olivia said, and hung up the phone. "What do you want, Avery?"

"Nothing, just wanted to know where your *scaredy cat* of a friend is.", Avery said.

Olivia clenched her fists, then said, "First of all, her name is Adelaide. Secondly, why do *you* care so much? And on the last note, she is not a *scaredy cat*, you are. Always scared of losing your popularity in school. That's why, you hung out with Julian, even though he didn't want to!"

Avery couldn't believe her ears. Nobody had said such things to her in her entire lifetime.

"Oh, almost forgot, you always took advantage of his kindness!", Olivia said.

"How dare you?", a fuming Avery said.

"What's going on?", Julian's voice came from the back of the group of students which had gathered around Avery and Olivia.

Upon hearing Julian's voice, the group parted, allowing Julian to walk towards them.

"Avery, what did I say yesterday?", Julian said. "The discussion is over!"

"I was just asking Olivia about Adelaide.", Avery said, feigning innocence.

"By calling her a *scaredy cat*?", Olivia said.

"You called her what?", Julian said.

Just then, all the lights went off at the same time, leaving all the lighting to the sunlight which was seeping through the windows.

While everyone was looking around, murmuring among themselves, a single light lit up, illuminating a single spot on the floor. Upon seeing the person standing in that single spot, a smile automatically appeared on Olivia's face, while Avery furrowed her brows.

"Adelaide?", Julian said.

"Julian, I'll never be able to make it up to you…. All the things you did for me, from saving me to standing up for me….", Adelaide said. "To making me have the most wonderful feeling by saying those magical words."

The moment Adelaide said this, both her and Julian could hear the series of gasps and murmuring. But that didn't stop Adelaide from continuing.

"Julian Atticus Wellington, maybe this quote in *'The Fault in Our Stars'* was written just for us…..",

Adelaide said. "I fell in love the way you fall asleep, slowly, and then, all at once."

The moment Adelaide finished speaking, the light went off, once again leaving all the lighting to the sunlight, but for just a few seconds. The lights then lit up together in the same manner they went out ; together. Teary eyed, Adelaide stood at the same spot from where she declared her eventual love for Julian.

Not being able to hold it any longer, Adelaide at once ran towards Julian, and leaped into his arms upon reaching. Julian's arms wrapped around her, while the crowd around them, except Avery and her group, erupted into cheers.

"I love you too.", Adelaide said.

Chapter – 6

The Prom, The Lesson, The Graduation, and The Surprise

Days passed by, and turned into months. Julian and Adelaide were closer than ever. And the fact that despite being in the same class, they kept their relationship at bay while studying, made it even more wholesome. From the day of their confession of love to each other to the last day of school, never once in their academics did they falter. And then, one of the days for which all the last year students had been eagerly waiting for, finally arrived.

"Mom, come on, I don't wanna be late to prom!", Adelaide called out from her room upstairs.

"Coming, honey!", Adelaide and Amelia's mother, Eleanor said. She was a pretty, middle-aged woman with a figure just like her two daughters, and straight, medium length brown hair tied up in a loose bun, with brown eyes, pale complexion, soft looking pink lips, and overall a beautiful appearance.

"I bet that today, all the girls in Dallas are in as much hurry as her. If not, more.", The girls' father, Adrian said. He was a middle aged man with a well built physique, short, wavy, blonde hair, green eyes, pale complexion, with his light beard carefully caressing his handsome, well defined, and sharp features.

"Totally.", Eleanor said. "And just as excited."

"Mom, come on up!", Amelia called out impatiently. "I'm not able to do it!"

"Julian could be here any minute.", Adelaide's voice came next. "Hurry up, Mom! It's urgent!"

"On my way!", Eleanor replied, and rushed up the stairs.

"And….done!", Eleanor said, having successfully zipped Adelaide's crimson prom gown, which was a beautiful piece of work, with golden flowery motifs embroidered on the lower side of the dress, along with being sleeveless. Adelaide's wavy, brown hair was let down, running across her back like a river, along with a few braids on the sides of her head, making her look absolutely stunning. The pearl choker around her neck with small round earrings added to her elegance.

"Just on time!", Amelia said, upon hearing the doorbell.

"I'll get it.", Adrian called out to the ladies upstairs.

Adrian opened the door to find Julian dressed in a black suit, with the pants and a tie of the same colour, along with a white shirt, the outfit perfectly bringing out his muscular body and broad shoulders.

"Right on time!", Adrian said. "Come on in."

"Thanks, Mr Matthews.", Julian said.

He didn't have to wait much for his date. Just after a few seconds, the moment Adelaide appeared on the top of the stairs, Julian felt like he skipped a beat just like the first time he laid eyes on his girlfriend. As she climbed down the stairs, he looked at her admiringly, lost in her beauty. And very soon, he found her in front of him, looking at him with the same admiration.

"So, are you ready?", Julian said, extending his hand towards Adelaide while bowing.

"As ready as I'll ever be.", Adelaide said, accepting his hand.

Julian straightened up, and said, "Shall we?"

"We shall.", Adelaide said, smiling.

As the couple were about to exit the house, Adrian said, "Have her back by eleven-thirty!"

"You got it, Mr Matthews.", Julian said.

"And the Prom King of the year is…….any guesses?", Mrs Perez, the Principal, said on the mic.

"Julian! Julian!", the crowd cheered.

"That's right! The one and only Julian Wellington, everybody!", Mrs Perez announced.

At once, Julian took Adelaide in his arms, with Adelaide saying, "Proud of you, handsome!"

The two then shared a kiss, after which Adelaide gave Julian a gentle push, while saying, "Now go!"

Adelaide then looked at her boyfriend being crowned the Prom King proudly, while being eager to hear the result for the Prom Queen.

After the crowd of the students settled down, Mrs Perez took over the stage once again, ready to announce the Prom Queen of the year.

"Now no guesses this time, alright?", Mrs Perez said. "Cuz this one is obvious…..our very own Adelaide Matthews, everybody!"

At once, the crowd erupted into cheers once again, with Adelaide not believing her ears. Nonetheless, she made her way to the stage, where she was then crowned the Prom Queen of the year, with her boyfriend looking at her just as proudly as she had been looking at him.

"STOP!", an angry voice echoed.

Everyone turned around to face the source of the angry voice, and found them to be none other than Avery Campbell.

"Just stop this nonsense, alright?", Avery said.

"Avery, you stop this nonsense.", Mrs Perez said.

"Yeah.", a female voice said from among the crowd. "Why are you spoiling the mood?"

Ignoring the question, Avery stormed straight to the bottom of the stage, and pointed her finger at Adelaide's crown.

"That crown…..is mine!", Avery said. "Just because the most popular boy in school made you his girlfriend doesn't mean you are the most popular girl in school! It's me! I'm the most popular girl in school!"

Julian stepped forward, but Adelaide stopped him.

"I got this.", she assured, then walked towards Avery.

"Well, you don't decide that, Avery.", Adelaide said, taking everyone by surprise. "The audience does."

Straightening herself up, Adelaide announced, "Whoever is in favour of me being the Prom Queen, raise your palm into the air!"

Then, looking at Avery, she announced, "And whoever is in favour of Avery being the Prom Queen, raise your fist into the air!"

The next moment, almost all hands with their palms open shot up into the air, and only Avery's group and only six other people with their fists in the air.

"What the….", Avery said.

"Got your answer?", Julian said.

"No no no!", Avery said. "This can't be!"

"But guess what, Avery.", Olivia said. "It is."

"But how?", Avery said.

"Everyone had enough of your arrogance, Avery.", Adelaide said. "That's how."

"But…but…", Avery stammered, but no words further came out from her mouth.

"Adelaide is right.", Mrs Perez said. "I've had many complaints about you from the freshmen and the sophomores, that you always bully them, and that you threatened them that if they ever tell me about you, then you would make their high school years miserable."

Avery looked at the Principal in complete shock.

"You might be thinking, then how did I come to know about this?", Mrs Perez said. "Well, it's because of your own self, Avery."

"Like Adelaide said, everyone had enough of your arrogance.", Mrs Perez continued. "And like I said, it's because of your own self. When some students from *your* year caught you tampering with the Prom royalty votes, then they approached me directly. And since they have had enough, they spilled all the beans about you that how you used to bully their younger siblings."

"Not only did I change the votes to their original form, I also purposefully held a meeting on the same day you and your friends went Prom shopping.", Mrs Perez continued. "With obviously not telling the attendees about the Prom royalty results."

"M…M…Meeting for what?", Avery said.

"Oh Campbell, I know you are smarter than that.", Adelaide said. "Obviously to discuss the ways to how to get back at you!"

A few days later on Graduation Day

"Remember the first day of twelfth grade, when we were looking forward to the yearbook, the prom, and this exact same day?", Adelaide said excitedly.

"How can I forget that?", Olivia said, her red hair tied up in a ponytail, which was then covered by her purple graduation cap. "Man, I can't believe that was almost a year ago!"

"I know, right?", Adelaide said.

"Okay, I'm gonna take her with me now. And just so you know, I've saved you a seat beside her.", Julian said, appearing behind his girlfriend.

Olivia at once showed a thumbs up to the couple, and proceeded to her seat.

Next moment, Adelaide felt Julian's strong hand gently grab her wrist, and pull her towards himself.

And then, she found herself sitting next to him, with a sea of heads wearing graduation caps in front of and behind her.

"The ceremony is about to start.", Julian said, then tilted himself towards Adelaide to whisper in her ear. "And I've always wanted to try that trick of pulling the girlfriend towards oneself."

"Well, you missed an important part of it.", Adelaide whispered back.

"I'll do that after the ceremony.", Julian said, winking.

Knowing full well that the missing part for Julian was to take her into his arms, Adelaide chuckled softly.

The graduation ceremony began shortly thereafter, with the procession of the school marching band, followed by the introduction by Mrs Perez and the school board, which was then followed by the guest speaker Mr Harris, and the former student Emily Sanchez. And then finally arrived the moment for which all the students had been eagerly waiting for. As expected, each student stepped up to the stage and received their high school diploma. But when a certain student stepped up to receive her diploma as well, the rest of the students at once erupted into murmuring.

Mrs Perez then gestured Avery to step up to the mic, for the girl had volunteered to speak in front of the graduating class, with the only ones knowing the reason for this unexpected request being Mrs Perez, and Avery.

"I know what you all must be thinking.", Avery said once she adjusted the mic. "That why am I here. Well, I have two things to say. Number one, I'll be forever grateful to the school board and Mrs Perez for giving me the opportunity to graduate, which I didn't think I could after all the awful things I did."

Avery then looked at Adelaide and Julian, saying, "And I'm here to apologize to all those whom I did wrong, the freshmen, the sophomores, my classmates, and most importantly, Adelaide and Julian."

As a reply, both Adelaide and Julian gave her a reassuring look, which encouraged her to speak further.

"I know that by merely saying sorry to individuals, I cannot undo the damage which I've done.", Avery said. "So that's why, I approached Mrs Perez, and she was the one who suggested me to do what I'm doing right now. She taught me that apologizing *does not* make you look weak. It helps improve your image in the mind of those you did wrong, strengthening you instead……and that's all I had to say, thank you."

After a moment of silence, the sound of a clap travelled through the hall, which was then gradually joined by various other claps, which eventually spread across each and every person in the hall.

"Oh, I'm so proud of you!", Eleanor said, hugging her elder daughter.

"Okay okay, now my turn.", Adrian said, hugging his daughter next.

"Congratulations, sis.", Amelia said.

"Thank you so much, guys.", Adelaide said. "I can't believe that I am an actual high school graduate now."

Amelia's gaze then fell on a number of reporters surrounding a man of around the same age as that of her Dad, with her sister's boyfriend standing next to him.

"Woah, Dr Raymond Wellington is actually here?", she said. "I thought you were bluffing!"

"Um, excuse me?", Adelaide said, raising an eyebrow.

"Hey, Dellie!", Julian called out. "Come here!"

"What?", Adelaide mouthed. "No!"

As a reply, Julian at once made his way through the group of reporters, and briskly walked towards his girlfriend.

"Good morning Mr and Mrs Matthews!", Julian said, upon reaching. "Good morning, Mellie! Do you mind if I take Adelaide with me? Just for a short while."

"Yes, of course!", Eleanor said.

"Sure!", Adrian said.

Having left with no option, Adelaide sighed, and was then led by Julian towards the reporters.

"Dad, I had like you to meet Adelaide, my girlfriend. Adelaide, my Dad.", Julian said, introducing them to one another.

"Pleasure to meet you, Dr Wellington.", Adelaide said.

"Pleasure to meet you too, young lady.", said Dr Raymond Wellington, a middle aged man with a head full of hair just like his son's, with the only difference being the white strands in some areas, with Adelaide noticing the stark resemblance between the father and son.

"Julian, I gotta go.", Raymond said, checking his watch. "I have a very important meeting."

"Okay Dad, see you.", Julian said.

"Congratulations to you both once again!", Raymond said, walking away.

"Thanks Dad!"

"Thanks Dr Wellington!"

Julian and Adelaide said in unison.

Just then, Adelaide felt a tap on her shoulder, and turned around to find Avery.

"Avery?", Adelaide said.

"Uh….um, I'm sorry.", Avery said.

"Sorry? For what?", Adelaide said.

Avery looked at her confusingly.

"You already said that back in the hall.", Adelaide said, smiling. "Sorry for what now?"

"But….", Avery said.

"No buts.", Adelaide said. "Come here."

Saying this, Adelaide spread her arms, and hugged Avery for the first time.

Adelaide then looked at Julian over Avery's shoulder, who was smiling at her. Adelaide smiled back, and then pulled apart from Avery, only to find her teary eyed.

"Woah, I've never seen you cry. Nor that I want to, now.", Adelaide said. "Go on, your family is waiting for you."

"Thanks a lot, Adelaide, for everything.", Avery said, wiping her tears. "You too, Julian."

Once Avery was gone, Julian said, "And now, the important part."

Saying this, Julian pulled Adelaide towards himself, taking her in his arms.

"Julian! My parents are still here!", Adelaide said.

"Don't worry, they are busy chatting with Olivia's parents.", Julian said.

"But the others are still here!", Adelaide said, and pulled apart from Julian.

"It's a good thing you did that.", Julian said, and put his hand inside his pocket. "I have to show you something."

He then took out a small, square shaped red box with golden motifs on it, along with blunt edges.

Adelaide realized what it was, and a soft gasp escaped her lips. Julian opened the box with his hands, and Adelaide saw the beautiful oval cut white diamond ring nestled inside it.

Next moment, Julian was on his knee, holding the small ring box in front of Adelaide, who could feel her heart summersault inside her chest, none of them noticing the people who had gathered around them.

"Adelaide Grace Matthews, will you make me the happiest person on the Earth?", Julian said. "Will you marry me?"

Tears spilled down Adelaide's cheeks, and she nodded.

"Yes!", she said, and the next moment, the crowd around them erupted into cheers and claps, just like the time when Adelaide had confessed her love for Julian.

Next moment, Julian stood up, took out the ring from the box, took Adelaide's hand into his, and gently pushed the ring down her ring finger.

Chapter – 7

All Good Things

Julian and Adelaide were beyond happy when their parents decided to conduct their wedding in one of the largest wedding halls in Dallas, with the ceremony to be conducted a week after Julian's proposal to Adelaide.

On the wedding day, the hall was decorated exquisitely, with chairs abundant enough to seat all the relatives and friends from the side of both bride and groom.

While standing at the end of the aisle, Julian waited impatiently for his bride to arrive. But he was not the only one waiting. The best man Liam Wellington stood with Julian, along with the relatives and friends of the bride and groom, who sat on either side of the aisle, waiting for Adelaide to emerge from the door with Adrian.

And after a few more seconds, the doors opened, and out emerged the beautiful bride with her father. She donned a beautiful white wedding gown, with sleeved laces, and a long, embroidered veil starting from her head, going along her back, and onto the floor, where it flowed just like a river when she walked. The wedding outfit also consisted of a festoon necklace which consisted of pink rubies, along with matching earrings. Adelaide's hair was tied up in a beautiful, wavy bun, which was held along with the veil using a beautiful matching tiara.

The arrival of the bride embarked the playing of the melodious bridal processional music, with everyone turning around to get a view of the bride.

Upon reaching the end of the aisle, Eleanor took her daughter in her arms and kissed her on her forehead, after which, Adrian placed Adelaide's hand in Julian's hand. The groom then escorted the bride to the podium, with the Maid of Honours, who were none other than Amelia and Olivia, holding the flower basket and Adelaide's bridal bouquet respectively, while the bridesmaids consisted of Adelaide's cousins, as well as friends.

"So, are you ready?", Julian whispered.

"As ready as I'll ever be.", Adelaide whispered back, with the reply being the same as the one on the day of their prom.

A few days after the wedding, Julian and Adelaide started exploring colleges in Dallas itself, so that they could remain close to their families, and to each other. Little did they know that something entirely different was about to unfold in their lives.

One day, while taking their usual evening stroll on the nearby street, Adelaide started feeling dizzy, which she assumed to be just sleepiness, as she had woken up too early that day, for she and Julian had to meet the admissions manager of a college. The dizziness soon disappeared, but was very soon taken over by weakness.

"Are you okay?", Julian said. "I mean, it's okay to be dizzy because you woke up early today, but weakness?"

"I don't get it. I've never felt like this in m.....", Adelaide began, but then her surroundings started to blur and a certain heaviness took over her body completely.

Luckily, Julian caught her in his arms when she lost consciousness, preventing her from hitting the ground.

___

"What's the matter, Mom?", Julian asked worriedly. "Is she okay?"

"You really don't have any idea, do you?", said Dr Natalie Wellington, who, like her husband, was a successful doctor, with the only difference between them being that Raymond was a brain surgeon, while Natalie was a gynecologist. She was a beautiful, middle-aged woman with a petite figure, shoulder length, straight auburn hair, dark blue eyes, pale complexion, and pink lips.

"What do you mean?", Julian said.

"Let's just say that Adelaide got lucky that her mother-in-law is a gynecologist.", Natalie said.

After a few seconds of pondering, the realization hit Julian.

"You...you mean to say that she is pregnant?", Julian said.

Natalie smiled, nodding.

"Oh my God.", Adelaide said softly. "I'm pregnant?"

"Yeah.", Julian said, just as softly. "How are you feeling?"

After a few moments of silence, when there was no reply from Adelaide's side, Julian grew worried, and said, "Dellie?"

"Huh?", Adelaide said.

"Are you okay?", Julian enquired.

"Yeah.", Adelaide said in a low voice, tears streaming down her cheeks.

"Hey, it's okay.", Julian said. "Don't you get sad."

"Sad?", Adelaide said. "Who said I'm sad?"

"But you were just….", Julian began, but was interrupted in between by Adelaide.

"Crying?", she said, finishing Julian's sentence.

"Yeah.", Julian said.

"Well, I just can't believe that there is a baby inside me.", Adelaide said. "I mean, I've dreamt of two things for a long time now. One of them got fulfilled. And the other one is about to be."

"Two things?", Julian said.

"Yeah.", Adelaide replied. "One for a loving husband, and second, a healthy little baby in our arms."

"Oh my…..", Julian said. "I can't believe this!"

"I know, me too.", Adelaide replied.

"Dellie, we are gonna become parents!", Julian said, now tears streaming down his cheeks too. "I am pretty sure that I'm the happiest person in the world right now!"

"Wrong. We are the happiest *persons* in the world right now.", Adelaide said, smiling.

Chapter – 8

The Unexpected

One could say that Adelaide and Julian were ecstatic for the arrival of their baby, and the fact that after several efforts, they both had been accepted for an online degree in one of the best colleges in Texas, made it even more wholesome.

Various instances in the pregnancy, such as the baby's first glimpse in the ultrasound, hearing it's heartbeat, it's first kick and the movements, and 'it's a girl!' made their joy know no bounds, despite the frequent morning sickness. The expecting parents were also thankful that their baby was healthy and happy, which she used to confirm from time to time in the ultrasound, as well as through her kicks. And the nine months went by just like that.

One day, while everyone was busy in their own affairs, the sound of a loud thud came from the room of the expecting parents, followed by a loud scream. Putting all their works on halt, Julian and his family at once ran up to the room, only to find

Adelaide writhing in pain on the floor, with the bedside table fallen a few feet away from her.

"She is coming!", Adelaide whimpered. "The baby is coming!"

Adelaide could feel her pain becoming more intense as she put all her strength in pushing the baby out.

"I can see the head.", Natalie said. "Come on, honey. You can do it."

Adelaide shut her eyes, her grip on Julian's hand becoming tighter.

"Ahhhh!", Adelaide screamed as she pushed one more time, her hair stuck to her forehead due to all the sweating. And then finally, it was over.

"She is here.", Natalie said in a low voice.

In the very next moment, the beautiful, melodious sound of the newborn's wailing filled the room.

Adelaide looked at the small wriggling human in her mother-in-law's arms, and her pain subsided the next moment.

"Chelsea….", Adelaide whispered softly.

"She is perfect.", Julian said, and looked at Adelaide to find her looking back at him.

"You did it, Dellie!", Julian said, and kissed his wife on the forehead. "You did it!"

Natalie took the baby and had her cleaned and wrapped up. But just as she was about to put Chelsea into her mother's arms, Adelaide felt a sharp pain in her stomach. She looked down and found the bottom half of her hospital gown drenched in blood. Natalie seemed to have noticed this too, for she immediately handed over the baby to the nurse and sat down on her previous position in which she helped deliver Chelsea.

"Dellie?", Julian said, and his eyes fell on the blood drenched gown. "ADELAIDE!"

"Julian, you need to get out of here, right now!", Natalie said.

"Mom, what's happening?", Julian said, deeply distressed.

"I don't have time, Julian!", Natalie said. "And neither does Adelaide, if we don't take her to the ICU right now!"

Julian paced continuously outside the ICU, waiting for his mother to come out. But when his patience got the best of him, he could not help but peak into the room through the little window on the ICU door.

On seeing the sight of his beloved wife inside the ICU, with all the tubes going through her body, with she lying lifeless in there, Julian felt numb, and all the sounds of his surrounding subsided completely. He suddenly started feeling hot, with beads of sweat appearing on his forehead.

"Julian?", said Amelia, who was sitting with her parents outside the ICU.

"Huh?", Julian said.

"You need to sit down.", Amelia said. "Come on."

Saying this, she led him to the chair and made him sit down.

"Here, have some water.", Adrian said.

Julian still couldn't believe that his in-laws were being nice to him. After all, it was because of him that their daughter was in this condition, or that's what he thought.

"Dad, your daughter is in that room because of me.", Julian said.

"Okay, then answer me this.", Eleanor said. "Did you want any of this to happen?"

"What?", Julian said, taken aback by the question. "No!"

"Okay. So did you do anything in the labour room to trigger that bleeding?", Eleanor said.

"No Mom, why in the world would I do that?", Julian said.

"Then how can you blame yourself for all this?", Eleanor said.

"I…..um……it's….", Julian stammered, but was unable to speak.

"Just because you are the father doesn't mean it's your fault.", Eleanor said. "It was a complication, which can happen to anyone."

"Don't worry, son.", Adrian said. "Everything will be alright."

After a few more minutes of waiting, a teary eyed Natalie finally came out with her team.

"Mom?", Julian said. "How is Adelaide?"

"You all may go now.", Natalie said to her staff, who looked at Julian.

"I said, please go.", Natalie said. "I need to do this alone."

A few seconds later, when all the ICU staff members were gone, Natalie turned towards Julian, and opened her mouth to speak, but no words came out of her mouth. Instead, the tears which were threatening to spill from her eyes upon her exit from the ICU were now streaming down her cheeks.

She shook her head slowly, and fell in her son's arms.

"No…..no, it can't be.", Julian said. "It can't be."

He then pulled apart from his mother and without any warning, stormed into the ICU.

"Julian, wait!", Natalie called out. As she was about to go after him, Eleanor kept her hand on her shoulder.

Natalie turned around to face Eleanor, saying, "Mrs Matthews?"

"Let him be.", Eleanor said. "He needs to have some alone time with his wife."

"But Mr and Mrs Matthews, your daughter…….", Natalie began, but was stopped midway by Eleanor.

"I know.", she said, tears streaming down her cheeks too. "We will see her after Julian."

"But……", Natalie said, but couldn't complete her sentence.

Upon entering the ICU, Julian found Adelaide's lifeless body on the bed, with the tubes still there. Her eyes were closed, as if she was just sleeping, with the dreamy green iris underneath the eyelids and the long eyelashes.

Knowing that she would never wake up, he sat down beside her lifeless form, and gazed at her as if for the first time.

"How could you do this to me, Dellie?". Julian said. "How could you leave me like this?"

He then took her hand in his, and placed a soft kiss on it.

"You didn't even hold our baby.", Julian said, his already red eyes brimming with tears. "And college? We opted for that online degree just for Chelsea. How could you leave her?"

"Your parents won't accept it, but I know it's my fault.", Julian continued.

After a few more minutes of gazing at his wife, after expecting deep down for her to wake up any minute, Julian stood up, and wiped his tears. And that's when it struck him, he had forgotten the most important thing.

He leaned in, bringing his face close to Adelaide's face, and touched his lips to her slightly parted ones.

After the kiss, he straightened up, and as he turned around, he heard a beep, only to find that the source of the beep was none other than the patient monitor, which upon his entrance had been showing only straight lines, with them being replaced by various wavy and zig-zagged ones. Having been grown up around doctors, Julian could easily make out that the green, zig-zagged one was the ECG Strip ; the thin, wavy and yellow one was oxygen saturation waveform ; the wide, wavy and green one was the respiratory waveform.

Julian then looked at Adelaide, whose chest was heaving, despite her eyes being still closed.

"MOM!", Julian shouted, and stormed out of the ICU in the same manner he had entered.

"Julian?", Natalie said. "What's the matter? Why are you shouting?"

"Mom, you *need* to go in there.", Julian said. "Adelaide is *breathing*!"

"Honey, I think you need to have some rest.", Natalie said.

"Mom you gotta believe me!", Julian said.

"Bro, you are hallucinating.", Liam said, having reached the hospital a few minutes ago. "Just sit down."

"Okay, you all think I'm hallucinating, right?", Julian said. "Just come and see for yourself."

Saying this, he gently grabbed his mother's wrist and took her into the ICU.

"Julian, I'm telling you there is no wa.......", Natalie began, but paused abruptly when she saw the sight in front of her.

A few seconds later, Natalie rushed out of the ICU, and began yelling the names of her staff members, startling everyone by the sudden change in her behaviour.

Chapter – 9

The Complete Family

A few hours ago, when Julian informed everyone outside the ICU that Adelaide was breathing just minutes after his mother declared her dead, they all thought him to be hallucinating, but the reality was something else entirely.

Natalie and her team at once rushed into the ICU after Julian proved to his mother that there had been no hallucination from his side.

A few minutes later, Natalie emerged from the ICU, with her face bearing an amazed look.

"Mrs Wellington?", Eleanor said. "What happened?"

"Honestly speaking, I don't know.", Natalie said. "I mean, this has never happened before."

"Mom, what has never happened before?", Liam said.

"Julian, you were right!", Natalie said, and hugged her elder son.

"Can someone explain to me what's happening here?", Amelia said.

Natalie pulled apart from her son, and moved towards Amelia.

"Amelia, your sister…..she…..", Natalie said, unable to control her excitement.

"Adelaide what, Mrs Wellington?", Eleanor said.

"Mrs Matthews, Adelaide….she is alive!", Natalie said. "And she has opened her eyes as well!"

"What?", all the people present there said in unison, except for Julian and Natalie.

"I knew it!", Julian said. "I knew that she would never leave me!"

"We are gonna transfer her to the recovery room.", Natalie said. "You all can meet her there."

"How are you feeling, honey?", Eleanor said.

"A little sour, but fine.", Adelaide said, smiling. "Don't you worry, Mom."

"I'm sorry to interrupt, my ladies, but there is someone who had like to meet you.", Julian said, and entered the room the very next moment.

Adelaide's eyes fell on the small bundle her husband was delicately cradling in his arms.

"I'll come back later.", Eleanor said, having already met her little granddaughter. "Chelsea would want to have some alone time with her parents."

Saying this, she exited the room, gently closing the door behind her.

"Wanna hold her?", Julian said.

"Is that even a question to ask right now?", Adelaide said. "Of course!"

Julian chuckled, and the newborn was then very gently and smoothly transferred into her mother's arms, who cradled her in her arms with utmost care. And the moment Adelaide held her daughter in her arms, the tears which had no existence a few seconds ago, spilled from her eyes and down the cheeks.

"She is beautiful!", Adelaide said.

"Just like you.", Julian said, gazing admiringly at Adelaide.

Adelaide looked up at Julian, who then leaned forward and placed a soft kiss on Chelsea's forehead, which caused the baby to stir in her sleep. Julian then kissed Adelaide in the similar manner, thankful to have the love of his life back.

"You know, I'm so thankful that you are here with us. You don't know the state I was in when you almost……", Julian began, but paused midway when Adelaide kept her free hand on his mouth.

"Let's just forget about what happened, alright?", she said. "What matters most is that, our family is complete."

"Copy that.", Julian said, smiling.

The couple looked at their sleeping daughter, who had the hint of a smile on her face.

"Welcome to the world, Chelsea Jane Wellington.", Adelaide spoke softly.

9 789888 927729 45